Every new generation of children is enthralled by the famous stories in our Well-Loved Tales series. Younger ones love to have the story read to them, and to examine each tiny detail of the full colour illustrations. Older children will enjoy the exciting stories in an easy-to-read text.

The Gingerbread Boy

retold for easy reading
by VERA SOUTHGATE, MA B Com
illustrated by ROBERT LUMLEY

Ladybird Books Loughborough

THE GINGERBREAD BOY

Once upon a time, there was a little old woman and a little old man. They lived by themselves in a little old house.

They had no little boys and no little girls.

One day, the little old woman said to the little old man, "I shall make a little boy out of ginger-bread."

"I shall make his eyes from two fat currants. I shall make his nose and mouth from bits of lemon-peel. I shall make his coat from sugar."

So the little old woman mixed the gingerbread. She cut out the little boy's head, his body, his arms and his legs. She patted them out flat on a baking tin.

Then the little old woman put two fat currants for his eyes. She put bits of lemon-peel for his nose and his mouth.

She made his coat from sugar.

The little old woman put the gingerbread boy into the oven to bake.

"Oho!" she cried. "Now I shall have a little gingerbread boy of my own."

Then she went about her work.

Soon it was time for the little gingerbread boy to be baked.

As the little old woman went to the oven, she heard a tiny little voice. It said, " Let me out! Let me out! "

Then the little old woman ran to open the oven door. As she did so, out popped the little gingerbread boy.

The little gingerbread boy hopped and skipped across the kitchen floor.

He saw the door of the kitchen standing open and out he ran.

Down the street ran the little gingerbread boy. After him ran the little old woman and the little old man.

"Stop! Stop! Little gingerbread boy!" they cried.

But the little gingerbread boy only looked back and cried,

"Run, run, as fast as you can,
You can't catch me,
I'm the gingerbread man!"

And they could not catch him.

The little gingerbread boy ran on and on. Soon he met a cow.

"Stop! Stop! Little boy!" said the cow. "You look very good to eat."

But the little gingerbread boy only ran faster.

"I have run away from a little old woman and a little old man," cried the little gingerbread boy. "I can run away from you, I can."

"Run, run, as fast as you can,
You can't catch me,
I'm the gingerbread man!"

And the cow could not catch him.

The little gingerbread boy ran
on and on. Soon he met a horse.

"Stop! Stop! Little boy!" said
the horse. "You look very good to
eat."

But the little gingerbread boy
only ran faster.

"I have run away from a little old woman, a little old man, and a cow," cried the little gingerbread boy. "I can run away from you, I can."

" Run, run, as fast as you can,
You can't catch me,
I'm the gingerbread man!"

And the horse could not catch him.

The little gingerbread boy ran on and on. He began to feel very proud of his running. "No one can catch me," he said.

Just then he met a sly old fox.

"Stop! Stop! Little boy!" said the fox. "I want to talk to you."

"Oho! You can't catch me!" said the little gingerbread boy and he began to run faster.

The fox began to run after the little gingerbread boy. The little gingerbread boy began to run faster still.

As he ran, the little gingerbread boy looked back and cried, "I have run away from a little old woman, a little old man, a cow and a horse. I can run away from you, I can."

"*Run, run, as fast as you can,*
You can't catch me,
I'm the gingerbread man!"

"I don't want to catch you," said the sly old fox. "I just want to talk to you."

But the little gingerbread boy kept on running. And the fox kept on running.

Soon the little gingerbread boy came to a river. He stopped at the river bank and the fox came running up.

"Oh! What shall I do?" cried the little gingerbread boy. "I cannot cross the river."

"Jump on my tail," said the fox, "and I will take you across the river."

So the little gingerbread boy jumped onto the fox's tail.

The fox began to swim across the river.

Soon the fox turned his head and said, "Little gingerbread boy, you are too heavy for my tail. You will get wet. Jump up on my back."

So the little gingerbread boy jumped onto the fox's back.

The sly old fox swam a little further out into the river.

Then he turned his head again and said, "Little gingerbread boy, you are too heavy for my back. You will get wet. Jump onto my nose."

So the little gingerbread boy jumped onto the fox's nose.

Soon the fox reached the other side of the river. As soon as his feet touched the bank of the river, he tossed the gingerbread boy into the air.

The fox opened his mouth and snap went his teeth.

"Oh dear!" said the little gingerbread boy, "I am one quarter gone!"

Then he cried, "I am half gone!" Then he cried, "I am three-quarters gone!"

And after that, the little gingerbread boy said nothing more at all.